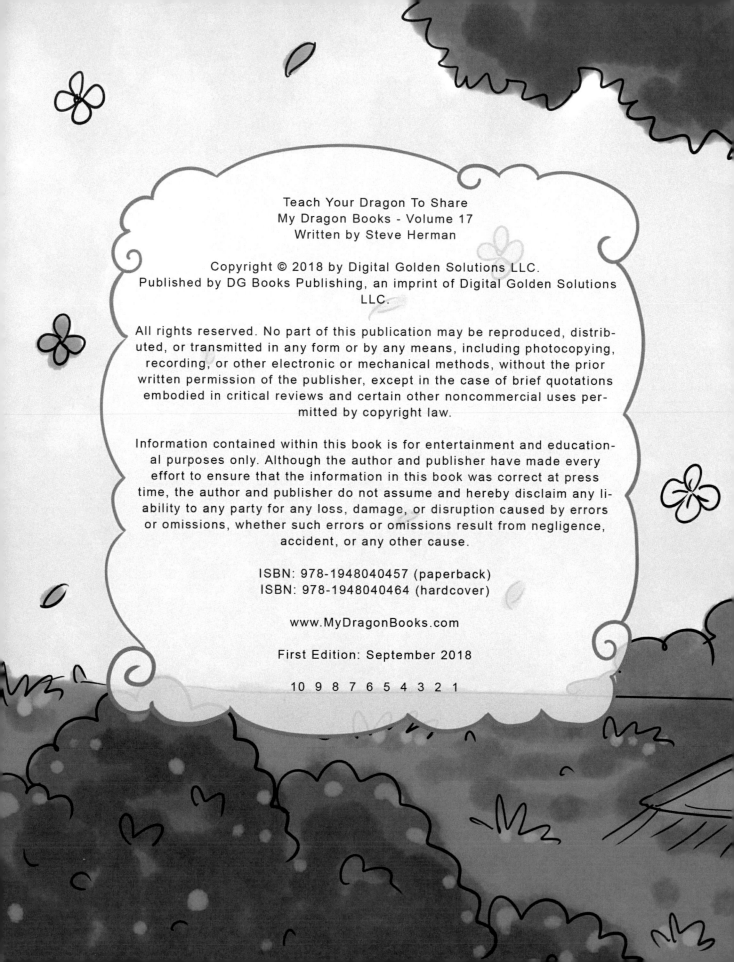

Teach Your Dragon To Share
My Dragon Books - Volume 17
Written by Steve Herman

Copyright © 2018 by Digital Golden Solutions LLC.
Published by DG Books Publishing, an imprint of Digital Golden Solutions LLC.

All rights reserved. No part of this publication may be reproduced, distributed, or transmitted in any form or by any means, including photocopying, recording, or other electronic or mechanical methods, without the prior written permission of the publisher, except in the case of brief quotations embodied in critical reviews and certain other noncommercial uses permitted by copyright law.

Information contained within this book is for entertainment and educational purposes only. Although the author and publisher have made every effort to ensure that the information in this book was correct at press time, the author and publisher do not assume and hereby disclaim any liability to any party for any loss, damage, or disruption caused by errors or omissions, whether such errors or omissions result from negligence, accident, or any other cause.

ISBN: 978-1948040457 (paperback)
ISBN: 978-1948040464 (hardcover)

www.MyDragonBooks.com

First Edition: September 2018

10 9 8 7 6 5 4 3 2 1

Since Diggory Doo was little, he needed to be taught... About the things that he should do and things that he should not.

He learned to play with toys,
to be careful not to break them,

And clean up all his messes
whenever he would make them.

He learned to mind his temper
and not look for stuff to burn –
The list was rather long
of all the things he had to learn!

Not too long ago,
before Diggory learned a better way,
He kept the toys all for himself,
so no one else could play.

"I'm all alone," cried Diggory Doo,
"and I'm not having fun;
Everyone has lots of friends –
I'd be happy with just one!"

Mother baked an apple pie and set it on the shelf – Diggory saw it sitting there, and ate it by himself!

Diggory aced his spelling test,
and he was feeling swell –
Instead of sharing his good news,
he chose not to tell.

He kept the hurt all bottled up
and bore it all alone –
His buddies could have cheered him up
if they had only known.

When other friends asked to help, he told them, "Go away!" So while Diggory Doo was working, the others went to play.

"Share your toys with other kids, and they will share theirs with you."

"When you have an apple pie,
give everyone a slice,"

"Then they'll split their treats with you –
Doesn't that sound nice?"

Diggory scratched his head and said,
"That's good advice, no doubt;
You've never steered me wrong before;
Okay, I'll try it out!"

It wasn't always easy,
and sometimes he'd forget,
But Diggory learned his lesson
about how to share, you bet!

"Drew," he said, "I now can see
that sharing's worth the trouble,
For when you share the good things,
your happiness will double."

"But when it comes to duties
or the sorrows that you bear,
You can cut them right in half –
Just remember you must share!"

"Get your FREE Gift from Diggory Doo at www.MyDragonBooks.com/gift"

Read more about Drew and Diggory Doo!

Visit
www.MyDragonBooks.com
for more!

Made in the USA
Middletown, DE
30 November 2020

25766644R00027